# My Teacher
# Sleeps in School

# My Teacher Sleeps in School

BY
**Leatie Weiss**

ILLUSTRATED BY
**Ellen Weiss**

FREDERICK WARNE · NEW YORK LONDON

*To Gary, who always knows where teachers sleep,*
*and to all my students in Hawthorne, New Jersey,*
*who were never quite sure.*     —L.W.

*To Katie, Susu, and Peter.*     —E.W.

Text Copyright © 1984 by Leatie Weiss.   Illustrations Copyright © 1984 by Ellen Weiss.

Frederick Warne & Co., Inc.   New York, New York

LIBRARY OF CONGRESS CATALOGING IN PUBLICATION DATA
Weiss, Leatie.
My teacher sleeps in school.
SUMMARY: Because Mrs. Marsh is always in her
classroom before the students arrive and always
stays after they leave, Mollie becomes convinced that
her teacher has no home other than the school.
[1. Teachers—Fiction.   2. Schools—Fiction]
I. Weiss, Ellen, ill.   II. Title.
PZ7.W44814My 1983      [E]        83-10427

ISBN 0-7232-6253-5

1 2 3 4 5 88 87 86 85 84

PRINTED IN THE U.S.A. BY RAE PUBLISHING CO., INC.   BOOK DESIGN BY BARBARA DU PREE KNOWLES

"Good-bye," called Mrs. Marsh. "I'll see you all tomorrow." Mrs. Marsh went back into the school, and everyone began walking home.

"I think the teacher sleeps in school," said Mollie. "I think she stays there all night long."

"What a dumb idea," said Gary. "Teachers don't sleep in school."

"Mrs. Marsh does," said Mollie. "She's always there when we come. And she's always there when we leave. I think the classroom is her house."

"Why don't you ask her?" dared Gary.

"I did once," said Mollie, "and she just laughed and laughed. But she didn't say yes or no."

"But where would she sleep?" said Gary. "Where would she eat?"

"Let's look around the room for clues tomorrow," said Mollie. "Maybe we'll find out."

The next day Gary could hardly do his work. He kept watching Mrs. Marsh and wondering. "What if it's really true?" he whispered to Mollie. "What if she really lives here?"

Pretty soon Lisa and Jason were wondering too.

"Where does she keep her clothes?" asked Jason.

"In the closet, of course," said Lisa. "Behind the paste and paper."

At play time, when Mrs. Marsh wasn't looking,
they opened the closet door.

"Look!" whispered Lisa. "A towel! And soap!"

"And a mirror!" squealed Gary.

"I'll bet she gets dressed in this closet," said Mollie.

"And *undressed*, too," giggled Lisa.

"I'll bet she wears funny pajamas," said Gary.
"And gloppy cream on her face," said Jason.
They pictured Mrs. Marsh in her pajamas and
couldn't stop laughing.

Next, they tiptoed over to the play kitchen.

"I saw her hide two bags here this morning," said Mollie.

"More proof!" said Gary in a loud whisper. "It's paper plates and napkins and lots of forks and spoons. She must be having company."

"I see cake mix and eggs in this bag," whispered Lisa. "She must be baking a real cake."

"I think she cooks her supper here every night," said Mollie.

"That oven is only make believe," said Jason.

"She can make it work," Mollie said. "Teachers can do *anything*."

Then they thought about where
Mrs. Marsh ate her supper,

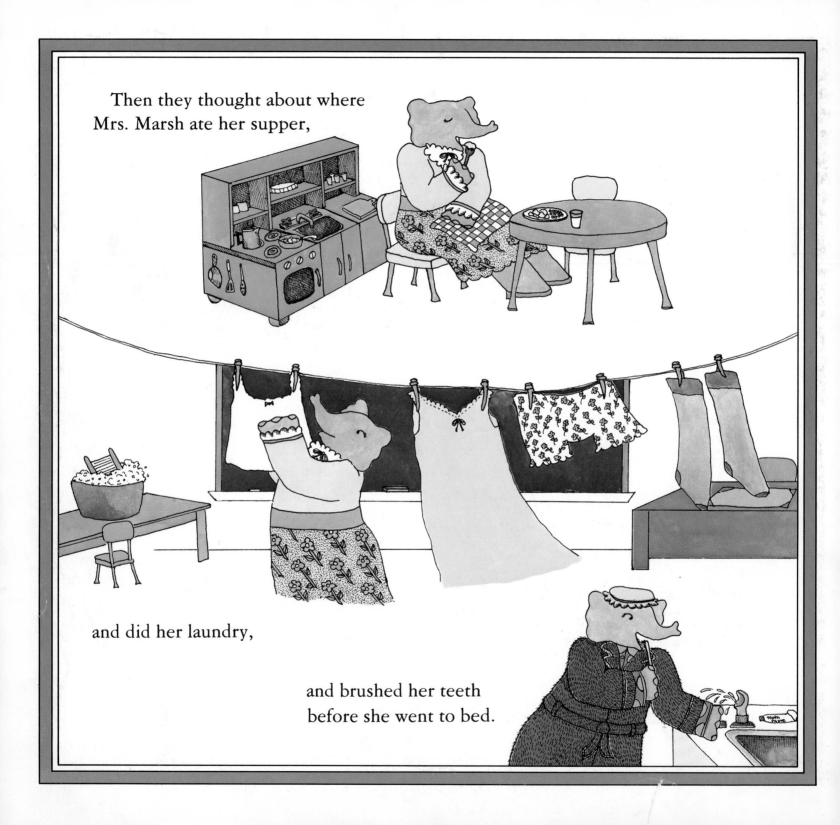

and did her laundry,

and brushed her teeth
before she went to bed.

But where did she sleep? That was still a mystery.

"Maybe she sleeps on the bookshelf," suggested Gary.

ZZZZZZ

"Or on the piano," said Mollie.

They looked and looked, but they couldn't find any clues.

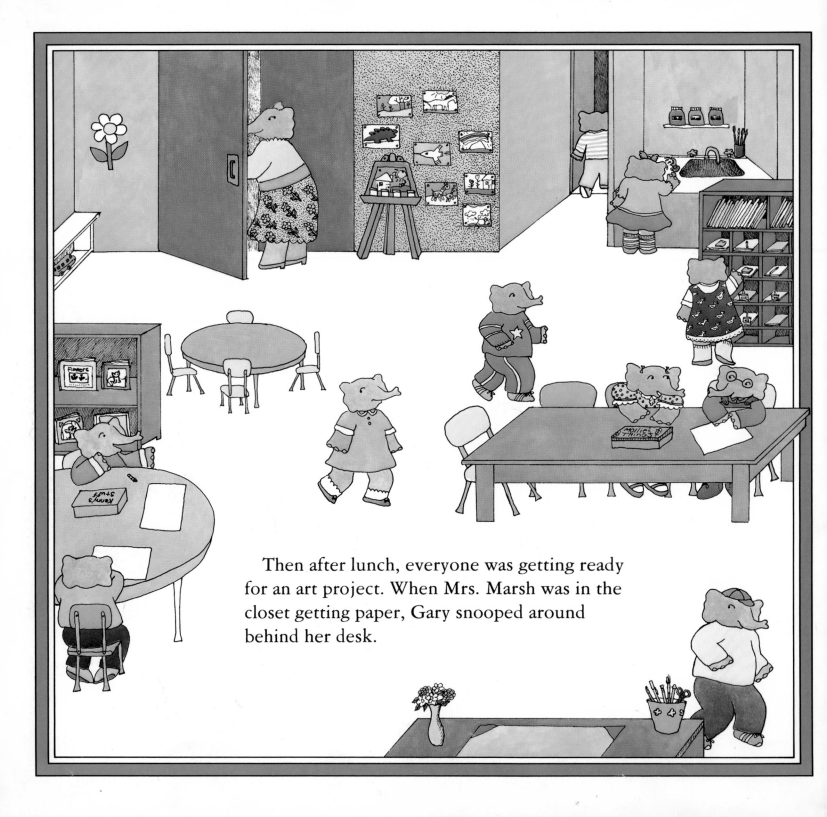

Then after lunch, everyone was getting ready
for an art project. When Mrs. Marsh was in the
closet getting paper, Gary snooped around
behind her desk.

"There's something under here!" he whispered. "Come and see!"

"A pair of slippers!" said Mollie. "And a pillow! She must sleep under her desk. We never thought of that!"

"I told you so," said Gary. "She really *does* sleep in school!"

"Poor Mrs. Marsh," sighed Lisa. "I bet it's lonely here at night."

"And creepy," said Jason.

Then Mollie had an idea. "Let's leave her a good-night snack," she said.

"And a nice note," said Jason.

"And something cuddly to sleep with," said Lisa.

Gary had part of a sandwich left over from lunch. Jason had saved six potato chips for later. Lisa got the teddy bear out of her cubby. Mollie was in charge of the note.

"Surprise!" she wrote. "We know you sleep here. Good night—sleep tight."

Gary promised to keep everything a secret, but soon the whole class knew. Everyone started giggling and whispering.

Mrs. Marsh looked puzzled. "What is going on here today?" she asked.

But nobody answered.

By three o'clock, Mollie had wrapped up the good-night package. Then Gary sneaked it under Mrs. Marsh's desk.

The next day everyone got to school early. They could
hardly wait to hear what Mrs. Marsh would say.
  But all she said was, "We're going on a mystery trip
today." And she wouldn't tell them where. Not even a hint.

Everyone got on the school bus.
They rode and rode.

At last they stopped at a
white house with a blue door.

"This is where I live," announced Mrs. Marsh.
Gary looked at Mollie. Mollie looked at Lisa. Lisa looked
at Jason. Then they followed Mrs. Marsh inside.

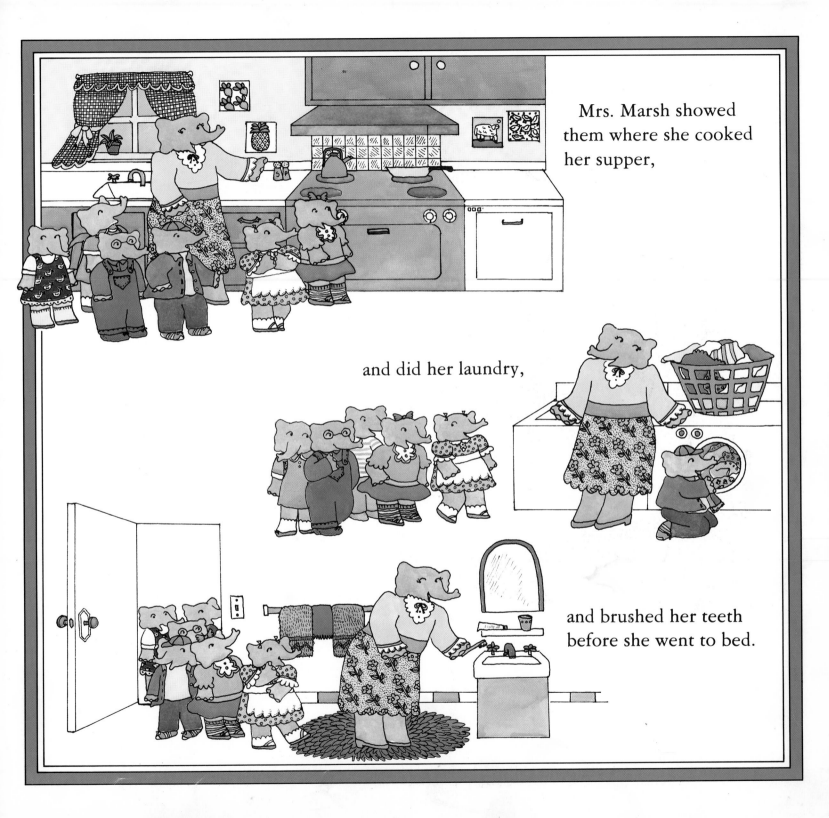

Mrs. Marsh showed them where she cooked her supper,

and did her laundry,

and brushed her teeth before she went to bed.

"And this," said Mrs. Marsh, "is where I sleep."
"Every night?" asked Mollie.
"Every night!" said Mrs. Marsh.
Then she showed them her children's rooms.

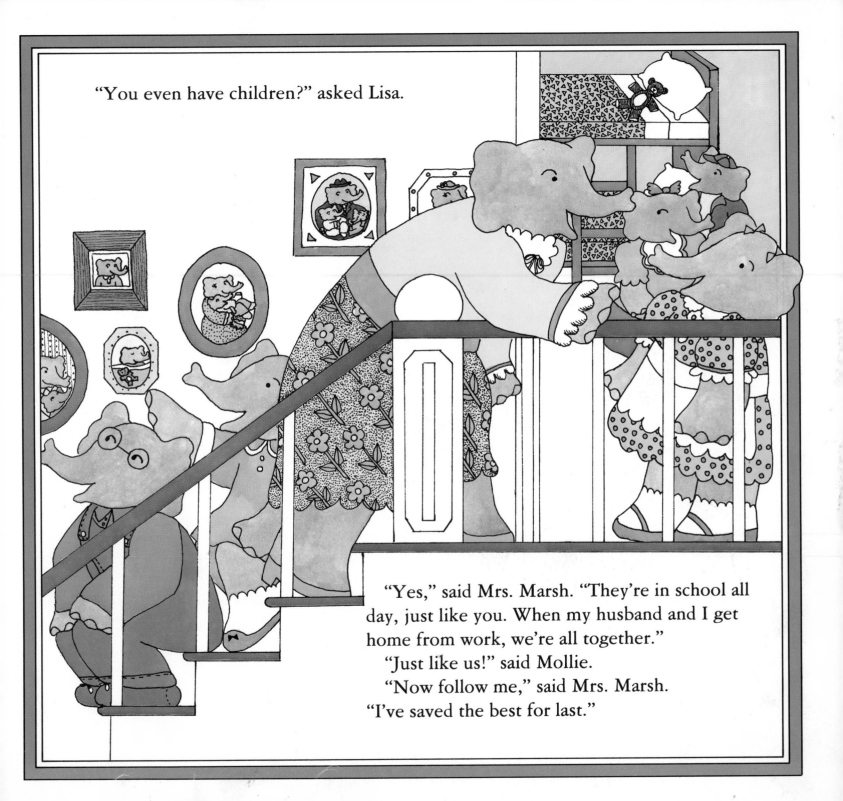

"You even have children?" asked Lisa.

"Yes," said Mrs. Marsh. "They're in school all day, just like you. When my husband and I get home from work, we're all together."

"Just like us!" said Mollie.

"Now follow me," said Mrs. Marsh. "I've saved the best for last."

She led the class into the dining room.
There were the paper plates and napkins
from the shopping bag at school!

"I've been planning this special treat for
the class," said Mrs. Marsh.

"Oh," said Mollie, "we thought . . ."

"I know what you thought," Mrs. Marsh
said, laughing.

Then Mrs. Marsh brought out a big cake,
and just like Mollie's note, it said "Surprise!"
"I baked this last night," said Mrs. Marsh.
"I baked it in my own oven, in my own
kitchen. And after that I went to sleep
in my own real bed."

Gary gave Mollie a poke. "I knew it all the time,"
he bragged. "Teachers *never* sleep in school!"
Mollie didn't even answer him.

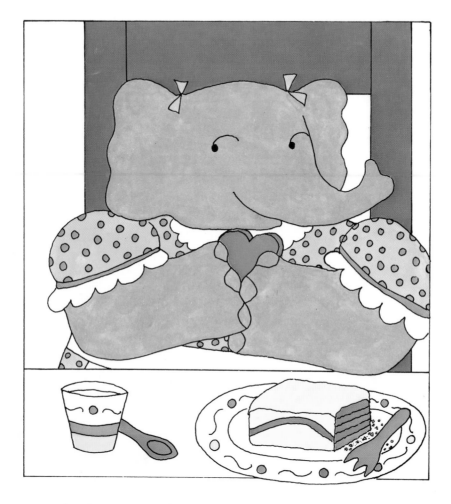

And she saved the biggest heart for Mollie.

Mrs. Marsh was smiling at her in a special way. "Mollie,"
she said, "would you help me cut the cake?"
Mrs. Marsh served everyone a piece with a heart on it.